# Twin Sisters

by

# Cassandra Deluca

# Twin Sisters

For information address: mickiedaltonbooks@lycos.com

First Published in 2016 in Australia

ISBN: 978-0-9944523-7-5

*Published by The Mickie Dalton Foundation*
*NSW*
*Australia*

*www.mickiedaltonfoundation.com*

# Twin Sisters

It was cold and damp outside. There was a good view from my window. You could see down the hill to the beach, the sun hadn't risen yet. There were a few birds in the sky. Coming up the driveway was my Mum and JD. JD's our dog, Mum takes him for a walk every morning before getting ready to go to work. It was six in the morning and the sun was starting to come through my window. My bedroom is the only one facing the beach.

I had to fight my sister for this room. My sister and I are twins, we've both got really long blonde hair that reaches our bottoms, it's curly as we both just had it permed not long ago. We are about 5'4" tall, thin, blue eyes. The only difference was that Trisa is into heavy metal, Harley-Davidsons and bikies, whereas I'm into surfing and guys with tanned skin, muscles, great bodies and also into surfing.

Sometimes people get Trisa and me mixed up, and so they work out the differences. Every morning I go down to the beach for a surf and Trisa sleeps in. We've only been living here for a month now and the school holidays are coming up. Trees and I have only one year left at school, we turn 18 in the holidays. Trisa is half an hour older than me. We don't stick around each other much. At birth, Mum couldn't think of any names for a girl so when her two sisters walked in to greet her, she decided to call us after them, Trisa and Linda.

"That's what I will call them," Mum said.

The only way Mum and everybody else could tell us apart was by giving us charm bracelets. Trisa got a gold one and I got a silver one, so that any time they got confused they just looked at our bracelets. A couple of times we changed the bracelets and Mum went mad when she found out. We used to wear the same clothes until we reached high school and went our separate ways. Trisa surfs occasionally and has a great tan too, you can see she had to learn how to surf because sometimes Mum would only let one of go out at night and if the other one had something on, the other one would have to pretend that they were the other person.

Why Mum was like that we don't know, probably because Dad left us when we were young. Dad had fallen in love with a young woman that was good friends with Mum. Dad is 6'7" tall with dark brown hair, handsome, and big build, only because he uses weights all the time. Our Mum is six feet tall with reddy-brown hair. Mum used to surf on her days off. Mum is a real estate agent and also works as a model for Hot Tuna, so we get all our surf clothes cheap. The other kids at our school were really impressed with the clothing, as we got all of the new designs before they went into the shops.

I decided to get out of bed and go down to the beach before getting ready for school. I went to my wardrobe to choose what to wear that day when Trisa waltzed into my room.

"Hi Trisa," I said. "Why are you up so early? You don't normally get up until eight o'clock and it's only 6:30."

"I've got to ask you a favour, Linda."

"What do you want this time, Trisa?"

"Well Linda, you go have your shower and then I'll come for a walk to the beach with you."

"Okay, but what have you got planned for me this time, Trisa?"

I finally chose my denim jeans, three-quarter Hot Tuna top and my Hot Tuna jacket. I grabbed them all along with my towel and underwear then I headed to the bathroom. After I'd finished my shower and got dressed I heard a knock at the door then Mum yelled out, "Linda, you in there?"

"Yes Mum," I said and opened the door, still brushing my teeth.

"Linda, I have to go away for the weekend, Hot Tuna have arranged for me to go to Sydney and stay there to model the new swimwear to be on sale for the holidays. So that means I'll be gone for four days. I'll be leaving tomorrow, which is Friday as you know and I won't be coming back until Monday. Now Linda, you and Trisa will be all right now won't you?"

"Yes Mum," I said.

"Oh and Linda, I've left some money on the fridge for you and Trisa. Also, there's some money in the cookie jar for food and groceries if you run out of anything."

"But why are you telling me now Mum, if you're not leaving until tomorrow?"

"Because Linda, I am leaving about three or four o'clock in the morning and won't be able to tell you tonight.

I haven't told Trisa yet. But if I forget to tell her, make sure that you do, okay Linda?"

"Yes Mum."

"Well, I'm going to go and get breakfast ready."

"Okay Mum."

"Oh and one more thing, Linda."

"Yes Mum."

"Make sure that Trisa doesn't have any of her outrageous parties while I'm gone, okay?"

"I'll try my best to stop her, Mum, that isn't always easy."

"I understand Linda, but do your best."

After I'd finished brushing my teeth and done my hair I start to go back to my room when Trisa jumped out from behind me.

"Trisa," I said. "Stop doing that! Now, what have you got planned?"

"Well I was going to ask you to do something for me, but since Mum is going away it doesn't matter now."

"How did you know that Mum was going away?"

"Well Linda, I was just on my way to tell you to hurry up in there but Mum had beaten me to it. I was listening to what she was saying but Mum didn't see me. She must have thought I was still in bed."

"Well, I'm on my way to the beach, so you may as well come along Trisa, and tell me anyway. At least now I don't have to explain everything to do you about what Mum has just said."

"Hey, would this be a great whole weekend to ourselves and also the whole house. I can't wait till tomorrow now, Linda."

We both walked down to the beach, Trisa never saying another word until we reached the sand. We walked over to the table and chairs set there for barbecues. As we were seated, Trisa started talking again.

"Now Linda, what I wanted to tell you is that tomorrow Mum's thinks I've got this date with a surfy. You see, Mum had set me up with one of her friend's sons. Mum thinks it would do me good to be with somebody that is well brought up instead of being around the people I'm usually around."

"So Trisa, what do you want me to do, then?"

"Well you see, Linda, there's this party tomorrow and Ross, one of the guys had invited me out but I really want to go to the party. Anyway, anything is better than hanging around a wax head who talks about the wave they caught that morning."

"But what's that got to do with me, Trisa?"

"Well Linda, if I don't go on this date with Dave, Mum said she'll stop me from going out in the summer holidays."

"Still, what's that got to do with me?"

"Well Linda, I want you go on the date with Dave while I go to the party with Ross. So you see, even though Mum is going away, I'll still have to go on the date I just remembered. So will you do it Linda, please?"

"I don't know Trisa. I think Mum is right, besides I don't like blind dates."

"Don't worry, Linda, you'll get along with him. After all, you're into that sort of stuff, you know the first wave of the day and all the rest of the stuff that goes with that kind of thing."

"Let me think about it. I'll let you know tomorrow."

Trisa didn't say any more about Dave or the date as she knew that if she kept on about it I wouldn't do it. We decided to head home and by the time we got home, Mum had breakfast ready and waiting on the table for us.

"Trisa, I've got something to tell you about this weekend," she said.

"Don't worry Mum, Linda has already told me everything."

"Well then girls, I'm off to work. Don't be late for school, don't forget to go to school tomorrow, after all it is the last day before summer break."

"No we won't forget, Mum," we both said.

Trisa and I answered at the same time, we did that a lot, after all we were identical twins. We ate our breakfast and grabbed things together and started for school.

"Today we'll have to take our own cars," Trisa said.

"Why?" I asked, as we normally go to school in the one car. Trisa and I both got licences last year, on my birthday, and Mum bought both of us cars. Trisa also had a bike licence without Mum knowing. If Mum ever found out she would have shot Trisa. I agreed to take my own car and jumped in, but on the way to school I realised I had forgotten to fill it up, so I decided to do it after school finished. I had enough to get me there and back. I pulled up in the car park and got out. I looked around for Trisa's car but I couldn't see it anywhere yet. Trisa had left before I had, so she should have already been there before I arrived.

All day at school I hardly heard a word that was said, I was so busy worrying about whether or not to go on this date with Dave. The last period came which was English and Trisa was in my class as we both like the subject being identical twins which had some advantages. Anyway Trisa didn't show up. Mr Vincent asked me where Trisa was as she hadn't come to school the day. I thought that was really strange then I realised I hadn't seen Trisa once all day. I just said she was sick and left it at that. The bell rang the end of school, so I grabbed my things together and headed for my car. When I reached it, there was a note on the windscreen. I picked it up and opened my car. Once I was inside, I looked at the note. It looked like Trisa's writing, so I opened it up and read the contents.

> *"Linda,*
>
> *Sorry I didn't come to school today, on the way I ran into Dave and told them he was going on the date with you. I told him a bit about you and he agreed. But his Mum and our Mum will think it's me. Anyway, after I'd seen Dave, Ross came by and asked me to join them in this bike race, so I agreed. I wrote this letter and asked Dave to put it on your car for me. Dave agreed and left for work. I'll see you at home, whatever you do, don't let Mum know I haven't gone to school today.*
>
> *Love always,*
> *your sis, Trisa"*

After I read the note I put in my bag and started the car. I was driving home when I realised I needed to fill it up. It was on dead empty. So I headed back towards the garage, which was just a few seconds away, but when I reached the corner closest to the garage, the car just stopped and wouldn't start again. I got out and walked the rest of the way. When I reached the garage, a guy walked out to greet me. He was tall with sandy hair, really nice tan, great body, blue eyes and he had a really nice smile. I thought to myself that I could really fall for this guy. When we reached each other I introduced myself.

"Hi, I'm Linda, my car's run out of petrol down the road and I need some help. Could you please give me a hand to get it here for me?"

He said, "Hi, my name is Dave, whereabouts did you leave your car?"

"Just around the corner."

He agreed to help me after he had told his boss what he was doing, and he came back and we started walking towards my car. When we reached it, Dave had a funny smile on his face. I hopped in and Dave pushed my car to the garage. Once we reached it, I thanked him and filled up with petrol. Then I went to pay for to the fuel. I reached into my handbag to get my purse when the letter from Trisa fell out. I bent down to pick it up but Dave had beaten me to it. He looked at the letter as he was handing it back to me. I thanked him again and asked him if he could throw the note in the bin for me, as I didn't need it any more. He just nodded and threw the letter away. I paid him the money and walked out. On the way back to the car, Dave yelled behind me.

"You're Linda, right?"

I nodded.

"And your sister's Trisa, right?"

I nodded again and got back into my car and headed home. When I got there, Trisa was waiting out at the front. I pulled up and got out and started heading inside when she stopped me.

"Linda, you didn't say anything to anyone, did you?"

"What about, Trisa?"

"You know, about the letter I wrote you."

"Oh no, I haven't told anyone anything."

"Promise not to tell Mum."

"I won't Trisa, now stop worrying."

"So Linda, did you decide whether or not you're going on the date with Dave or not tomorrow?"

"Well, I've been thinking about it all day and..."

"And what did you decide?"

"Well, I decided yes, I will go. If that Dave's anything like this Dave I met today then I'd gladly go along with you."

"Oh Linda, you're wonderful, thank you!"

We both went inside. Mum wasn't back yet so I decided to get changed and go down to the beach for a surf before she got home. I went to my room and changed into my wetsuit. I grabbed my board as well as my towel and my Hot Tuna jumper with a hood. I went downstairs and picked up my car keys just as the phone rang. Trisa answered it. Straight away she looked at me and said, "Yes," so I hesitated. She was just listening and then she said "Hang on," and asked me where I was going. I pointed to my board and said, "Down to the beach," and Trisa said "Bye" to me and kept talking on the phone. I jumped into the car and headed for the beach. It took only a few seconds to get there, I took my board and headed down the path.

The tide hadn't gone out yet so I started towards the water. After a while, the tide was heading back but there were still some good waves. I decided to just sit there for a while on my board then I looked up. I could see somebody coming up the beach also with a board and in their wetsuit. I knew it was a guy but I hadn't had a good enough look to see who it was. He put down his towel and headed for the water. He was coming towards me and as he was getting closer I realised it was Dave from the garage.

"Hi," I said. "I didn't know that you surfed."

"No," he said. "I didn't know that you did, either."

"Well, now we both know, don't we?" I said. "Do you live near here, Dave?"

"Yes," he replied. "I live up on Richey Crescent with my Mum. She's a fashion designer, she designs swimwear and designer clothing, you know, all that sort of stuff. So where do you live, Linda?"

"Well, if you look straight up that hill to the two-storey house, well, the window that you can see on the top floor is my room, my sister's room's on the other side."

"So you don't have to come far, then?"

"No I don't."

"How come if you live on the beach, well nearly on the beach and you still drive your car down?"

"Well," I said. "It's easier than carrying your board all the way, besides sometimes I decide not to surf and just swim or sunbake, so I leave my board on the car. So do you own your own car, Dave?"

"You, I do. I own a four-wheel-drive, Toyota LandCruiser. It's nothing special but it's mine. I'm planning on getting another car but I haven't saved up enough money yet. I don't rely on Mum for money all the time, I prefer to have my own money to be independent, you know what I mean."

"Yes Dave, I do. Do you always come surfing here or at the beach near your house?"

"Well, I have to confess that this is the first time I've been to this beach to surf. I always surf the beach near my house."

"Well what made you surf here today, then?"

"Oh, I was just talking to this girl earlier and she said something about this beach."

"What did she say about this beach?"

"Just that you'd be here."

"How did anybody know I'd be here, no one knew except for Trisa. Do you know my sister, Dave?"

"Yes I do."

"How do you know her?"

"Well, you see my Mum knows your Mum, remember when I said my Mum designed swimwear?"

"Yes."

"Well, your Mum models it."

"And is your Mum going to Sydney tomorrow, too?"

"Yes, that's right."

"Well then, have you always worked at the garage or just started there? I've never seen you there before!"

"Well to tell you the truth, I just started there today. You see I have only just finished the mechanics course and Mac, my boss employed me to work for a while anyway, while his mechanic was on holidays. But that's enough about me. So how's school going?"

"Pretty well, I'm just started to get settled in and tomorrow is the last day before summer break. So Dave, what are you doing for the summer break?"

"Well Linda, I have to work unless Les comes back!"

"Who is Les?

"Les is the mechanic I told you about that I'm replacing at the moment. Why, what are you doing for the summer break, Linda?"

"Oh, I'm not sure yet, I haven't really decided on what I want to do."

I looked to see if he had a watch on, as mine was in the shop getting repaired. Dave noticed I was looking at him strangely and asked me what the matter was. I explained about my watch and asked him for the time. He said that it was 5:30 and asked me why I wanted to know.

"Well you see, Mum hadn't got home when I arrived home myself, so I decided to come to the beach, well until teatime, anyway."

So I started heading towards the shore on my surfboard when I noticed that Dave was also heading back. Once we were dry, I started to head home. When I noticed Dave didn't have his car here, I offered him a ride home and he accepted.

When we reached Dave's house it took me by surprise. It was beautiful. It had an oval driveway that went all the way around the front door and back towards the gate. The driveway also had lamps lighting it up and a big beautiful fountain in the centre. The fountain had a statue of a man in the centre with the water falling from his hands and his hat. His hands were reaching out as if to touch somebody.

The house was three storeys with a balcony on each level. Downstairs must have been the lounge room as the curtains were open and I could see a really big couch and a few chairs and right in the middle of the room was a large coffee table and above the table was a crystal chandelier hanging off the ceiling. I was thinking about how big his house must be when Dave said that he had an Olympic size pool at the back if I ever got sick of the beach and just wanted to swim in the pool. I thanked him and stopped at the front door. He asked me to come in and I refused and explained that Mum would be getting worried by now if didn't get home. So he said goodbye and that he would see me tomorrow but the funny thing was we had never talked about tomorrow.

On the way home I kept thinking about him. I couldn't stop picturing his smile. He was gorgeous but I knew I'd never end up with a guy like Dave. When I reached home I pulled into the driveway thinking how plain our house seemed after seeing his house. I got out of the car and I was just about to take my board off the roof when I realised Dave's board was still on as well as his towel was in my car.

I decided to have a shower and get changed as well as have tea, then take Dave's stuff back to him. I thought that I'd better bring his board inside so that nobody could pinch it, as I knew I would be in trouble if somebody did and how could I ever explain that to him? I'd never forgive myself. As I walked inside, Mum was in the kitchen cooking dinner and I couldn't see Trisa so I walked up to my room. Trisa was coming out of the bathroom as I was going into my room. She noticed I had two surf boards and looked at me strangely and followed me into my room.

"Ha, Linda, what are you doing with two surf boards you only own one? So tell me, who owns the other one? How did you end up with it? And how long are you keeping it for?"

"Trisa, the board belongs to a guy I met today. His name is Dave. He works at the garage, he was surfing and I gave him a lift home after we finished. He forgot to take his board off my car."

"Oh yeah?"

"No, it is true, Trisa, I'm going to have a shower and get changed before I take the board back to him."

"You'd better have tea first, Linda, after all you know what Mum is like if you're out when she is ready."

"Yeah, I know."

She then walked out of my room and went back downstairs to the lounge. At home, Trisa spends most of her time in front of the television or in her room but in the summer she spends most of the time on the beach. Anyway I went and had my shower and by the time I walked back to my room Mum yelled out, "Linda, tea's ready."

"Yes Mum, I'll be down in a minute."

I got changed and headed downstairs. Once I reached the kitchen, I noticed there was a guy there talking to my Mum. I froze for a moment, thinking to myself that it was Dave, but when he turned around I realised it wasn't. Mum introduced me to him.

"Linda, this is Lea, Lea this is Linda."

We both said hi. I started to get really wobbly at the knees, so I sat down at the table. I couldn't believe my eyes, this guy was gorgeous, even better-looking than Dave. He was the same height as Dave, Lea had dark skin, brown eyes and brownie–blonde hair, sort of mouse colour. They both had the same cute smile.

Mum dished up tea and told Lea to sit down so he sat between Trisa and me, as they say, a thorn between two roses. But he was a definitely handsome guy. Trisa must also have taken a shine to him, as she too was blushing. Trisa always flirted with all the good looking guys. She would lead them on and then as soon as she had enough of them, she'd move onto the next one, whereas I was always too shy to even think about flirting with a guy.

Even though we were identical twins, you wouldn't think so with the way we did nearly everything opposite to each other. Everyone accepts that identical twins have the same likes and dislikes, to always wear the same things, to do the same things and to act the same way and in some cases, Trisa and I did but not all the time, only occasionally.

We finished tea and I told Mum I was going out for a little while as I had to return something to a friend. When Mum asked me to give Lea a lift home, I agreed and when Lea and I got into my car he thanked me for giving him the ride. I told me he was welcome as long as he didn't leave anything in my car. He just laughed and looked out of the window. I asked him where he lived and he told me Richey Crescent. I looked at him funny and drove him home. When I reached Richey Crescent I asked him, "Where do you live?"

"See that big three-storey house over there with the oval driveway?"

"Yes."

"Well, I live next door to that."

I was so relieved, thinking that Dave and Lea were brothers. After all, they looked a lot like, but there were some things different. Their eyes and a couple of other things about them made them look not the same. So I dropped Lea off at home and then went next door to return Dave's board. It was really strange as the feelings I had had for Dave, I had now for Lea as well. I knew there was no way I could choose between the two of them. I parked the car in Dave's driveway and got his surfboard and towel from my car. I headed towards the door but just then Dave started to come out. His eyes lit up when he saw me and so did mine. He explained that he was just on his way over to my place to pick up his board.

"I had to drop Lea off next door from Mum, so I was on my way over," I said.

Dave's eyes dropped to the floor any he looked really upset from what I just said.

"Did I say something wrong, Dave?" I asked.

"No not really," he said. "It's just that Lea and I don't get on."

"So you know Lea really well then?"

"Oh sort of," he said. "He's a real jerk, he is always thinking of ways to get a new girl, especially if I like one, he'll go out of his way to get her so I don't. He's weird in that way, not many girls stay with him for long. You see, he moves in on the girl, takes what he can get then quickly gets out before it's too late. He's 22 years old, he has no consideration, anyway talking about him makes me cranky, so let's talk about something better. So you're going on a date tomorrow, Linda?"

"Yes, but how did you know? Don't tell me, my sister told you right? Anyway, it's a blind dates and I hate blind dates as you never know whether or not you'll get along."

"Well, you get along with me now, don't you?"

"Well yes, but..."

"No buts. Blind dates aren't all that bad after all you might even know the guy."

"But the only Dave I know is you."

"Well, you never know your luck! So where are you going on the date?"

"I don't know, that reminds me. I don't even know what to wear."

"Just go as you are," said Dave. "If they don't like how you are, then there won't like you at all. What's the use of getting dressed up if you may never see this guy again? After all you don't have to impress anyone so that means you don't have to get dolled up, now does it?"

"No I suppose not, but I might end up feeling uncomfortable if I'm dressed casual and he's all done up."

"Well, for a surfy guy, I don't think he'll get all dolled up for a blind date now, do you?"

"No, I suppose not."

"Okay, let me take that board and my towel off your hands, talking about uncomfortable. You must be so uncomfortable holding that while you're standing there listening to me. Why don't you come inside and I'll offer you a drink to thank you for bringing my board back."

"Oh no, I couldn't intrude into your house, that will make me feel rude."

"Don't think of it, after all, I wouldn't have asked you if I didn't want you, now, would I?"

"Well, I suppose you're right. I'll just lock up my car," I said.

I did as I said then followed Dave into the house. He offered me a seat and asked me whether I'd prefer a hot or cold drink. I told him it didn't matter, so he said he'd just put his stuff in his room then make drinks. After he left the room, I started thinking about what he had just told me about Lea, and after thinking about everything, my feelings were turned back towards Dave again. After all, Lea didn't seem my type, I suppose I needed to hear something to make my mind up about who to choose, Dave or Lea. Now

I know it's Dave I want, after all it was Dave that I liked first anyway.

Then he returned with a cup of hot cocoa with a marshmallow and a spoon. He sat down next to me, we started talking about everything and anything but all the time I looked at my watch. It was nine o'clock, I stood up and told Dave that I had to go and I thanked him for the cocoa and for asking me in. He walked me to the door and opened the door for me. After he walked outside he walked me to my car. I said goodbye again. He asked me whether or not I would like to continue seeing him. I said yes, of course. I got into my car and drove home. Once I got home, Trisa asked me where I'd been.

I told her how I dropped Lea off and taken Dave's surfboard back to him, and we'd had a cup and talked. Also I told Trisa about how Dave asked me whether or not I'd like to continue to see him and how I'd said yes. Trisa confessed how she liked Lea and that she was jealous of me driving Lea home. I said that I wasn't interested in him and that I really liked Dave. I then decided to go to bed and said good night to Trisa. On the way upstairs, Mum called to me.

"Linda, don't forget tomorrow is the last day of school so don't forget to go."

"No Mum, I won't forget."

I headed to my room and when I reached it, I noticed my cupboard doors were open. Trisa must have gone through my wardrobe. I'd had to find out what she was up to. I got changed and jumped into bed. I sat there looking out of the window, thinking about everything that had happened today. I couldn't believe how much had taken place in just one day, I was looking at the beach trying to recall my day, just thinking for a while there I had a crush on Lea, until I found out what he was like. I couldn't believe somebody so good-looking would even want to be like that. But then again, Trisa was the same way. I was starting to get tired so I lay down and not long after my head hit the pillow I'd fallen asleep.

I woke up to the sounds of horns beeping at the front of the house. I looked out and saw it was still dark, so I got out of bed glancing at my clock and saw it was only three o'clock in the morning. I grabbed my robe and headed downstairs. Mum was outside packing her car with enough clothes to last a month. Mum always took a lot of things with her whenever she went anywhere, I suppose all women are alike. They wouldn't know what they'd end up wearing one day to the next. They'd always take one thing and the ones you left at home you really want to wear, so Mum took half a wardrobe with her instead. I'd always wondered what it would be like for Mum to find herself a boyfriend but I could never imagine it. Anyway I walked over to her and asked her if she wanted a hand.

"No it's all right," she said. "I only have one bag left to pack in the car."

"Who was beeping their horn?" I asked.

"Just some hoons driving past," replied Mum. "Knowing my luck, your sister knows them. I'm sorry I had to leave at such short notice, make sure your sister is up and dressed in time for school, after all I don't want you to miss a day while I'm not here, you never know what mischief you'll get yourself into. After all, I was a teenager once too, you know, and I know how you all think maybe different to me, but I still know what things you both could get up to without me around, and don't think I don't because I do. Remember, no parties while I'm gone and keep the house tidy, you can have a few friends over though no wild ones, okay? Ah well, I'd better start heading off or I'll never get there. I'll ring you as soon as I get there, the phone number's on the fridge if you need me for any reason."

"Okay Mum," I said. "I'm back off to bed because I have to get up again in a couple of hours. See you when you get back Mum, have a safe trip."

"And you both be good," said Mum.

"Yes Mum, we will, see you later, have fun."

"Yes darling, and you have some fun too, within reason. Bye. Oh, one more thing, don't forget to feed JD while I'm gone."

"No Mum. See you."

I turned around and headed back inside. I went back upstairs, went back to bed but just as I got into bed I realised I hadn't remembered falling asleep. Anyway, I was tired after the exhausting day I'd had yesterday so I set my alarm and went back to sleep.

As soon as the alarm went off in the morning I woke up and turned it off. I sat there for a while thinking whether or not I'd dreamt everything that had happened yesterday. Today, we all had to go to school to get report cards, the end of term grades, whatever you want to call them.

I got out of bed and went to check Mum's room, then I realised I hadn't dreamt it yesterday, it was all true and real. I headed downstairs and fed JD. Mum usually fed him except for when she was away. I put on the radio and got my breakfast. When Mum went away, Trisa usually skipped breakfast and was always planning something crazy. Somehow she always got me involved, like the date with Dave tonight for starters.

I started to worry about the date even more now, as it was tonight and I didn't even know this guy, let alone what time he was coming around. That reminded me to ask Trisa what time the date was.

I cleaned up the kitchen and Mum must have had breakfast before she left as there was a bowl and spoon plus a dirty coffee mug in the sink. After cleaning the kitchen, I decided not to go to the beach this morning and to have a shower and just wait for Trisa to get up and tell me more about this date tonight.

After I showered and changed, I knocked on Trisa's door. It was open a fraction. I thought she must have already been awake. I opened it and I couldn't see Trisa anyway, she must have left to go somewhere early this morning after Mum had left. This meant only one thing, Trisa was up to something but what? I thought to myself and that I'd better find out before she does whatever it is, which only meant one thing and that was trouble.

I went back downstairs and the phone rang. It was Lea. He asked me, "What are you doing tonight?"

I said, "I have a date with Dave."

"How is Trisa?" he asked.

"Okay," I replied.

"Can I talk to her?" he asked.

"I don't know where she is," I said. We talked for a bit more then I hung up. Something about the phone call had given me the creeps, but what I wasn't sure of was but it was as if Lea was trying to get either Trisa or me, but which one didn't seem to bother him.

It was time to leave the school, so I grabbed my things and headed off. I saw that Trisa still wasn't home yet. I thought she'd better get to school soon or Mum would be very shitty if she found out. On the way, I drove past the garage and looked for Dave. He couldn't have started work until later, so I drove to school where I parked my car and got out. I looked around for Trisa's car. Finally I saw it up at the back, so at least I knew she'd come to school. I went to my locker, got my stuff out but when I opened the locker door, Trisa came up behind me.

"Hi Linda," she said. "Sorry I wasn't home but Ross came round this morning and asked me to come for a ride with him, but when we went out, I realised how much I liked Lea and decided not to go to the party tonight and I told Ross. He wasn't too pleased but he said he knew it would happen."

"Oh yeah? Trisa. Lea rang up this morning and asked me what I was doing tonight."

"Yeah, and what did you say?"

"I told him I was going on a date with Dave."

"Yes, and...?"

"Well then he asked whether or not you were home and I told him you weren't."

"Lea was asking about me?"

"Yes Trisa, he asked if you were there, he also started asking things about you, too."

"Like what?"

"Like whether or not you had a boyfriend, how old you were, when would you be home, et cetera."

"So what did you tell him?"

"I told them no, you didn't have a boyfriend, I told him you were 17 going 18 soon, I also said I didn't know when you would be home."

"Oh wow, do you know what this means, Linda?"

"No, what does this mean, Trisa?"

"Well, it means that I like a surfy and he likes me, and it means that Mum will let me out all the time now like she lets you. It'll make Mum think I've started to grow up and out of my bikie friends, that's what it means. But first I have to try and see Lea."

"Somehow I think you will see him sooner than you expect to, Trisa."

"Oh yeah, you're still going on the date with Dave, aren't you, Linda?"

"I suppose so."

The bell then rang for first period. Trisa and I both had technical drawing with Mrs Jones so we headed for class. Mrs Jones is pretty cool, she lets us all talk in class and practically do what we want as long as we get our work done.

All day, Trisa and I had the same classes and instead of sitting next to our own friends we sat next to each other. The last class of the day came when Mr Harvey handed out all our report cards. They were sealed, the teachers sealed envelopes to make sure they would go to our parents.

Mum had gone away so Trisa and I decided to open ours when we got to our cars. The bell rang the end of term, we both headed for my car, once we reached it we opened our report cards. Mum said it had better be a good one or she won't give is a big 18th birthday party. We looked at our reports and compared them. Luckily, they were both good. We put them in our bags and got into our cars. When we got home, the phone rang. We both raced over to pick it up and in the end I left Trisa have it.

"Hello, who is this?" Trisa said. "Oh Mum, how is it in Sydney, what? Oh yeah we did, do you want us to tell you over the phone?"

Trisa picked up her report card and told Mum her marks then she past the phone to me.

"Hello Mum, how are things?"

"Hi baby, pretty good and how are you?"

"Good thanks, Mum."

"So tell me your results, Linda."

I picked up my report card and told Mum my marks.

She said, "I'm impressed with both reports. Well, I have to go now, Linda, bye darling."

"Bye, Mum."

Just as I hung up the phone, it rang again so I picked it up.

"Hello," I said

"Hello," said a male voice.

"Who's calling?" I asked.

"It's me, Lea. Is Trisa there?"

"Yes, hang on and I'll get her for you."

I handed the phone to Trisa and headed upstairs to my room. Once I walked in, I realised I had to work out what I was going to wear tonight. I didn't know who Dave was or what he liked, so I thought I'd better make a good impression. I then remembered Dave from the garage told me to wear something casual. I looked in my wardrobe and I couldn't decide, so I decided to have my shower first and do my hair before I worked on what to wear. I'd just got into the shower when Trisa knocked on the door.

"Linda, hurry up in there, I've got a date with Lea, I have to get ready."

"You'll have to wait a moment, as I just got in," I said.

"Well hurry up then, Linda, please."

I'd finished washing my hair and having my shower, I got out and dried myself when Trisa came back to the bathroom door.

"Have you finished yet, Linda?"

"Yes, I've just got to brush my teeth."

When I'd finished I went back to my room. I decided not to do my hair until I got dressed. In the end I decided on my violet dress, it was casual and dressy all in one. It was low-cut in the front and back, the dress went halfway down my thighs in between my knees and my bottom, with long sleeves. I grabbed my white sandals and my three-quarter white jumper.

Now it was time to do my hair. I decided to wear it up in a bun with a white and violet ribbon tied around it. I'd teased my fringe and added a hint of make up, just enough to make a difference but not enough to notice. To finish off, I sprayed my hair with some hairspray, added some deodorant and perfume. I looked at the clock and saw it was 7 PM. I hadn't had tea so I decided to take my wallet and some money to buy something when I was out with Dave.

Trisa waltzed into my room and I noticed we were wearing exactly the same thing. Luckily we were going to different places with different guys. The doorbell rang, so we decided to stay just the way we were. We went and answered the door together. It was Dave and Lea at the same time. Lea and Trisa left and I asked Dave in.

"Hi Dave," I said. "How come you're here, I've got a date with Dave."

"Yes that's me," he said. "There is no other Dave."

"Why didn't you tell me that it was you, then?"

"Because I didn't think you would go on the date if he knew it was me. By the way, you look wonderful."

"Thank you, so do you."

"Since you're all dressed up, we'd better go out then."

"Why?"

"We'll if you look that good just dressed casual, I can imagine what you'd look like dressed up."

"Why thank you, I never thought I'd made such an impression before."

"Well now you know that you do."

"So where are we going tonight?"

"It's a surprise, so have you had tea yet or not?"

"No not yet, I'd forgotten about tea so I decided to buy something when I was out."

"Well that's great then, because I haven't had tea yet and I was hoping that you hadn't either, so that we could have tea together."

"That sounds great! Let's go and get something to eat because I'm starving, are you?"

"Yeah, I'm starving too."

We walked outside and got into Dave's car. It was an all right car. Dave started up and we headed the town.

"So what would you like to eat, Linda?"

"I'm not sure, how about a hot dog and we can eat it while walking along the beach? How does that sound?"

"That sounds just about perfect to me," he said.

"I wonder how Trisa and Lea are getting along."

"I don't know," he said, "but I hope he doesn't hurt her."

"Me too, although Trisa might end up hurting Lea, she is known to do that too, you know."

"I suppose that we'll soon find out either way."

"Yeah, I suppose you're right."

We got our hot dogs from the fast-food restaurant and headed for the beach. Once we got there we found seats and sat down. We both ate our hot dogs without saying a word. I couldn't believe that all this time I was so worried about this blind date, when all along I'd known him already. I suppose in a way I was cranky at Dave for leading me on and not telling me that it was he, but on the other hand I was so glad that it was Dave and nobody else.

We finished our hot dogs and started walking along the beach. It was so funny, this was like a romantic walk on the beach but it felt as though there was something missing, I didn't know what. It just felt like something wasn't quite right, you could say it was just a feeling that I had.

"So what's the matter, Linda?"

"Pardon?"

"I said, what's the matter?"

"Oh, I'm sorry, nothing, I was just thinking."

"About what?"

"Oh, about how it was you all along and how you never said a word about it."

"Ah, but in a way I did, remember when you said that the only Dave you knew was me and I said you'd never know your luck."

"Yes, but..."

"So I sort of told you, didn't I?"

"Yeah I suppose you did in a way."

We kept walking a bit further when I realised that Dave had never told me where we were going tonight and he'd never been in any hurry to go anywhere.

"So where was it that you said we were going tonight, Dave?"

"Ah but I didn't."

"Well you had said it was a surprise."

"Yes, and it is."

"Well, tell me, please."

"Well really, to tell you the truth, there is nowhere."

"But you said it was a surprise."

"Yes and it is, even to me because I don't know where to and I hoped that you would have forgotten it even if I said it."

"But you honestly didn't expect me to forget now, did you? Why didn't you just say that you didn't know where we were going, and then we could have both talked about where to go and what to do?"

"Yes I suppose so. I'm sorry, Linda."

"That's okay, just don't do it again."

"No, I won't."

We just ended up walking further along the beach and then we went home. For some reason, it just didn't feel the way it should. There was no magic, like there was a wall between us.

Dave drove me home, we said good night and he left. I went into the lounge room to wait for Trisa to get home to see how things had gone with her and Lea. I hoped it had gone better than it did for Dave and me. For some reason, I just didn't feel the same for Dave any more. Why, I didn't know, maybe he was just not right for me.

I must have fallen asleep waiting for Trisa to come home as I didn't hear her come in. The last thing I remember was thinking about Dave and wishing Trisa would hurry up.

Finally I woke up to the sound of the door opening and she walked into the lounge.

"Hi Linda!" she said. "How did the date with Dave go? You must have got home early."

"Hi Trisa, the date was all right, yeah I did come home early. So how did things go with you and Lea? Where did you go?"

"Well it went great. Lea took me out for Chinese, he paid, I tried to but he wouldn't let me. Then we went to the movies, then to the beach. It was so romantic, he was so wonderful, we were going to come home but we decided that we'd better or we never get there. He dropped me off and went home."

"That sounds so good, so I you're going to be seeing him again?"

"Yes, tomorrow, and you're invited. So how did your date go, Linda? Tell me all about it."

"Well Trisa, after you and Lea left, I asked Dave in. We sat down for a few minutes then we left. He told me it was a surprise where we were going and wouldn't tell me, so we ended up just having hot dogs for tea and went to the beach and just talked. Then he dropped me back here and I was waiting to you to come home."

"Oh Linda! You poor thing, I'm so sorry, I didn't know. Well anyway, Lea's invited you and me to his house tomorrow, a big party. It's supposed to be really good, maybe you might meet someone there, even better than Dave. You really did like Dave too, didn't you?"

"Yeah I did a little but now I'm not so sure. I don't know whether or not I'll go to the party anyway, I'd be intruding on you and Lea."

"No, don't be silly, after all we wouldn't have asked you to come otherwise now, would we? You just have to come, Linda."

"All right, maybe just for a little while. I was kind of worried about you tonight with Lea, after what Dave had told me about him."

"Why, what did Dave say about him?"

"He said that Lea was a father three times to three 16-year-old girls and that he only uses girls. I didn't want to say anything but I couldn't help it, I just had to tell you."

"Yeah well, did you know that Dave and Lea are brothers, that Lea had been adopted out when he was a baby as his mother wasn't ready to have a child? Now Lea lives with his father and he has a different father to Dave."

"No, I didn't know that. Dave had told me that they didn't get along but not that they were brothers. How did you find out?"

"Lea told me, and Dave's a father, not Lea. You see, Dave was always jealous of Lea getting all the girls and then he made a couple of girls pregnant."

"Oh Trisa, how could I have been such a fool as to let Dave treat me like that? Why did he lie to me?"

"I don't know Linda, but I think that you should forget about him."

"Does Dave know Lea's his brother?"

"Yes, Dave knows, they found out when Lea moved next door a few years ago."

"Oh Trisa, how can I go to the party with Dave being next door?"

"Just forget about him Linda, he's not worth it."

I couldn't believe everything I just heard. Why would somebody lie to a person like that? I just don't know. I said good night to Trisa and went to bed. I lay awake for hours just thinking about Dave and everything that had happened in the last couple of days. I felt so stupid falling for Dave in the first place but he was good-looking and that explains why Dave and Lea looked alike.

At some point I woke up and looked outside. It was still dark. I was hoping that I had dreamt everything that had happened yesterday. I was so cranky that Dave had treated me the way he did. I thought about the party this evening and didn't know whether or not to go, but then I realised I had told Trisa that I would. Oh God, I felt depressed.

I lay awake all morning, I couldn't go back to sleep. I just hoped that this party wouldn't turn out like all the parties that Trisa went to or had. Maybe I could be wrong and the party would end up being a good one.

I spent all day at the beach, wishing that night wouldn't come. I tried to think of ways of getting out of going but I knew that there'd be no way that I could. When I got home, Trisa was all ready to go to the party and was trying to hurry me up. I told her to go and when I'd finished getting ready I'd meet her at the party. Trisa wasn't ready to go at first but I promised her that I go to the party straight after I'd finished getting ready. So Trisa left and I went to my room to decide what to wear. I chose my peach miniskirt with purple three-quarter top and bikinis and my white three-quarter jacket. I went and had my shower and got dressed, I braided my hair and teased my fringe. I put my white sandals on. I picked up my keys and left. In a way I was looking forward to the party now. But I was getting butterflies in my stomach and I hoped that I didn't have to see Dave.

I pulled up outside Lea's house and for a moment had second thoughts about going in but just as I was thinking of driving off, Trisa appeared beside me.

"Come on Linda," she said. "What are you waiting for? I've been waiting to you to show up, I was getting worried that you wouldn't arrive."

"Well I'm here now. Haven't you been in yet?"

"No, I've been waiting to go in with you."

"That's not like you, Trisa. Normally you're the first want to be there. What makes it so different this time?"

"I don't know Linda, maybe it's just Lea, he really makes me feel different. I just can't stop thinking about him. What is it about him?"

"Maybe you've finally started to turn around and let somebody like you?"

"I don't know. Anyway, that's enough about me, come on, let's get in there before Lea thinks I've changed my mind and stood him up."

I got out of the car locked it and walked into Lea's house. It was packed, it looked like everybody that lived around here was present. I kept an eye out for Dave, hoping I wouldn't see him but still in a way, I wanted to. What the party was for I didn't know. Trisa had gone off with Lea somewhere. I decided to get a drink and take a seat.

"What is a good-looking girl like you doing here all by herself?"

I turned around, startled and accidentally spilled my drink. I leaned forward to pick up the cup.

"Lucky they are not glass, eh?"

The whole time I realised I hadn't looked up to see who I was talking to, so finally I did look at the male figure behind me.

"Hi, my name is Tony," said the man. "I'm sorry if I startled you."

"No, that's all right, I was just daydreaming."

"So are you here with anyone or by yourself?"

"I'm here with my sister."

He sat down next to me and we were quiet for a while.

"Sorry, I didn't catch your name," he said.

"I didn't say it," I said.

"Sorry, I mean, what's your name?"

"Linda. So are you here with anyone?"

"No, I came alone. Do you know Lea, or have you just come here with your sister?"

"I came with my sister as I said, and yes, I do know Lea, he's seeing my sister."

"So what's your sister's name?"

"Trisa, we are twins."

"You must be pretty lonely here, then?" he said.

"Yeah, I am a bit. I was starting to wonder whether or not it was such a good idea coming in the first place. You see, I wasn't going to come but I promised Trisa that I would, so I had no choice."

"Well, Linda, I'm so glad that you did come along, because if you hadn't I wouldn't have been able to meet you."

"Well thanks. So you're a friend of Lea's, then?"

"You we surf together. Do you surf?"

"Yeah, often actually."

"So what have you got planned for tomorrow?" he asked.

"Nothing so far."

"Good, then..."

"What do you mean, good then?"

"Well I just want to ask you if you would like to go for tea tomorrow night?"

I was debating what to say when all of a sudden Dave showed up and came over towards Tony and me. But before Dave could say a word to me, I said to Tony, "That would be lovely! It's a date, then. What time?"

Tony said he would get to my place at 6 PM the next day and asked where I lived. Just as I finished giving Tony my address, Dave spoke up.

"Hello," he said and then to Tony he said, "You can go and get lost."

Tony turned to me and asked if I wanted to stay or go. I said it was all right and I would catch up with him later. Tony nodded and left.

"Hi Dave, what are you doing here?" I said. "I thought that you and Lea didn't like each other."

"We don't," said Dave. "Lea didn't ask me, I just came over as I'd seen your car at the front and I wanted to talk to you. I'd tried ringing you at home and there was no answer so I was going out to see if you were at the beach, then I realised that your car was at the front of Lea's so here I am."

"So what did you want with me, then?"

"I wanted to ask you over to my place for tea tonight to make up for last night. Would you like to do that, Linda?"

I was going to say no then I felt sorry for him so I ended up saying yes. Dave then said goodbye and that he'd better go before Lea found him there. I said goodbye and I told him I'd see him tonight. He started to walk away when I remembered I didn't ask what time.

"Dave, wait!" I said.

"What is it, Linda?"

"Oh.. um.. Make it 6:30 PM, okay?"

"Okay, bye."

"Bye."

After Dave had gone I started thinking. What did I do that for? I had made the date with Tony to get away from Dave but then I made a date with Dave as well. Oh I what have I done? I got up and went to look for Trisa. I couldn't see her anywhere so I walked to the front of the house but just as I reached the door I heard people talking so I headed towards the voices.

Then suddenly I saw Trisa and Lea. They were round the side of the house but they didn't see me. I heard Lea telling Trisa that he had to go away for a couple of days and when he got back he wanted to see her again. They seemed such a dreamy couple, they were wrapped in each other's arms, kissing and cuddling. I started to feel jealous because Trisa was so happy and I wasn't. Just as I was about to turn around and leave, Lea and Trisa saw me.

"Linda, what are you doing here?" said Trisa.

"I was just coming to find you," I said. "I was going to let you know that I'm going home now."

"You can't leave yet," she said. "The party is just starting."

"All right, I'll just stay for a little while, then I've got to get going."

"Trisa," said Lea. "I'll catch up with you soon and I'd better make an appearance before anyone wonders where I've gone."

They kissed each other again then he walked away.

"Linda, what's the matter?" said Trisa. "You look as if something is wrong. What is it?"

"It's Dave," I said. "He asked me to come over tonight for tea and I said yes, but just before that I told Tony that I would go out on the date with him tomorrow but I only told Tony that to make Dave jealous."

"Why on earth would you do that for, Linda? After all you're the nice person, you never offend anyone, never make anybody jealous. Why did you do it?"

"I don't know. I don't even like Tony but I suppose I'd better keep the date now, after all, like you said, I'm the nice guy."

"You never know, Tony may just end up better than you think."

"Or worse."

"Hey, or worse," agreed Trisa.

I stayed at the party for probably another hour then I said goodbye to Lea and Trisa and thanked Lea for inviting me over. Lea said it was his pleasure and tried to talk me into staying but I just said that I had to go. Trisa decided she'd stay for a while longer.

When I got home, I went upstairs to my room to try and decide what to wear. I wasn't sure how to dress for this evening. I started getting butterflies in my stomach after thinking about how bad the previous date had been.

After half an hour of debating what to wear, I chose a long pink dress which came to my ankles with straps instead of sleeves as it was quite warm tonight and I decided to wear my hair down and just pull back the sides with a headband made of pink and white lace. I wore my white scuffs. I thought this was appropriate enough to wear and to dinner without looking overly dressed. Finally I got myself ready and decided to put on a little make-up. It felt like I was trying to impress him but I didn't understand why.

I pulled up in Dave's driveway, unsure of whether or not to get out, but before I had time to decide, Dave was at my door. He was a real gentleman this time. He opened the door for me, took my hand and helped me out of the car and closed the car door for me. It all felt strange and yet exciting and it started to send tingles all through my body.

"Hello Linda," he said. "You look lovely this evening."

"Why, thank you Dave, you do too," I replied.

He was wearing blue denim jeans with a red coloured, button-up shirt with the top three buttons left undone, just enough to see his smooth, toned chest. It was starting to make me feel a little uncomfortable. As I looked up at him, I realised he was staring into my eyes with a dreamy smile on his face. He took me by surprise.

"Won't you come in and we'll have dinner?" he said.

"Yes, of course."

It felt like we had been standing there forever.

We went into the house and Dave took me straight into the dining room where the table was already set up with candles and glasses with champagne sitting beside the table in an ice bucket. It all looked like I had walked in on a romantic movie set. The light from the candles was flickering all over the room, the window was open to give a light breeze enough to move the candles flames, but not enough to put them out. There were also some flowers on the table, roses and carnations with a mix of Baby's Breath. It was very attractive with beautiful colours and aromas. I really did start to think that this night was going to make up for the other night.

Dave told me to take a seat that he had already pulled out for me. He disappeared a few seconds then returned to take his own seat and then a lady entered, carrying what looked to be our food. She placed the plates in front of us then left. I had thanked her before she had left the room. I started to wonder whether or not I should really be here but before I'd had time to think, Dave spoke.

"Linda, would you like a glass of champagne?"

"Only a little bit, please, but thank you," I said.

The food was beautiful. There was shrimp and calamari, fish with salad on the side covered in a white sauce. When we'd finished, the lady returned with more plates and she took away the first plates. This time there was fried rice with a mixture of red and white meat, a few fried vegetables, all marinated. It all tasted beautiful and then after that we got lemon meringue pie with ice cream.

I thanked Dave for all the wonderful food.

"It's nothing," he replied.

"I'm so sorry that your mother didn't eat with us after all the trouble she'd gone through," I said

"That wasn't my mother, that's Liz, our maid, it's her job to serve us. Have you had enough?"

"Plenty, thank you."

"How about we go outside to walk off our dinner?" he said.

"That sounds great," I replied.

We walked outside and ended up by the pool. It was indeed a rather large pool.

"You must really enjoy living here, Dave," I said.

"It's all right."

"My house looks tiny compared to yours."

"Yes, I suppose it does."

"Thank you for that wonderful dinner, but you didn't have to go to all that trouble."

"It's nothing, that's how we usually eat."

We walked around the pool and sat down under the gazebo which was a pretty shade of blue and underneath were two sun lounges, the same shade of blue. We sat there for a while saying nothing, just taking in all the scenery and smelling the fresh air. There was still just a light breeze blowing.

"It's a shame you never brought your bathers with you, unless you're up for a skinny dip," said Dave.

"It is a shame, but I would have to decline a skinny dip though, that's a bit too much for me."

"So what are you doing tomorrow, Linda? Any plans?"

"Actually I do have some plans," I replied.

"Really, and what have you got planned?"

"I made a date, I don't really want to go but it's too late to break it now."

"What do you mean, made a date?" he asked.

"Well early, when I ran into Tony he asked me out to dinner. I said yes but that was before you asked me over tonight."

"Can't you break the date?"

"Not really. Besides, I'd feel terrible if I did."

"Well, I suppose it's the right thing to do."

"Yes."

It was starting to get late so I said goodbye. Dave walked me to my car, he said he would catch up with me later. I drove home carefully thinking about the evening. When I arrived, Trisa still hadn't got home. It was just like her to stay out all night and then I'd have to cover for her. I was tired so I just went straight to bed.

In the morning I checked Trisa's room and there was no sign she'd slept in her bed, so I went downstairs to make my breakfast and there was still no sign of her. I was starting to worry about her. I thought that after breakfast I would go over to Lea's place and see if she was all right and still there. I got dressed and was just about to head out the door when Trisa waltzed in.

"Hi Linda," she said.

"Trisa, where have you been? I've been worried about you. I thought that something might have happened to you when I got up and you weren't here."

"I'm sorry," she said. "It's just that we were having so much fun that we forgot the time and by the time we did realise it was too late to drive home so Lea offered me a place to stay."

"Well as long as you're all right."

"By the way, how did your dinner go?" asked Trisa. "Was it another flop or was it better?"

"Actually he was quite the gentleman. He surprised me, he opened and closed doors me, we had a lovely dinner, then we just sat by the pool and talked until it was getting late, then we said goodbye and I left."

"Sounds a lot better than the first date. I'm glad things turned out a lot better for you, I was worried it would end up being another flop."

"Thanks, and how did your night go?"

"Lea's asked me to be his girlfriend. He is just so cool. I really like him, Linda, I like him a lot but I'm going to miss him though."

"Why, where is he going?"

"He's got to go to Hawaii on business."

"What is his job?"

"He's a photographer, sometimes he needs to travel on business, other times he stays here and takes photographs."

"So what sort of things does he photograph?" I asked.

"All kinds of things."

"So how long does he have to go to Hawaii for?"

"He's not sure, maybe a couple of days, maybe a week. He is not sure yet until he gets there. I'm really going to miss him, Linda."

"I'm so happy for you, Trisa. But I'm sorry that you've just got together now that he is going away."

I decided to go down to the beach for the day. Once I was there I took my surfboard off my car and headed for the waves. They weren't so bad today. I caught a few good ones but I got bored quickly though and decided to just sunbake a while. Once I was on the sand again I remembered that I had the date with Tony tonight. I wished I'd never made that date now, but I knew I had to go through with it.

Finally I decided to go home and get ready. I wasn't looking forward to it at all, I had butterflies in my stomach all afternoon, wishing tonight would never come. Of course, the time just flew by. I was upstairs getting dressed when the doorbell rang.

"Linda, your date is here," sang out Trisa.

"I'll be down in a moment," I called back.

Now I was really nervous. I was really starting to wonder why I did these things to myself. Finally I finished getting dressed. I decided on a Licic dress with long sleeves and low-cut in the back. It came all the way down to my ankles and I chose to wear my black high heels. I pinned my hair up on the sides and left the back of the hair just flowing down my back. Finally I made my way downstairs wondering why I'd gone to all this trouble, when all of a sudden I caught sight of Tony. He looked magnificent, better than I could ever have imagined. He had brown hair, brown eyes, a very masculine body and a beautiful smile. He was wearing grey slacks and a white long-sleeved top. He looked like a prince out of a fairy book coming to rescue his bride to be. I started to go weak at the knees, I forgotten that he was staring at me and I tripped on the bottom step. He raced over to grab me so that I wouldn't fall. I felt so embarrassed.

"Are you all right, Linda?" he asked.

"Yes, thank you."

He could obviously see the embarrassment in my face, so he quickly said, "You look very lovely tonight, you don't scrub up too bad at all."

"The same with you. I mean, you don't look too bad yourself."

Now I was starting to feel awkward, wondering why Tony made me feel all these different things all the time, it made me feel as though I was a little schoolgirl wondering whether or not I'd be kissed for the first time.

"So what have you got planned for me this evening?" I asked.

"It's a surprise," he said.

I remembered when he said that to me before and I felt a bit depressed.

"Why the long face?" he asked. "You still want to go out now, don't you?"

"Oh yes," I replied. "It's just that the last time somebody said that to me it was a surprise, it ended up not so good."

"Well I'm sure this will make up for it, Linda," he said. "After all, I have already planned everything. I was more worried you'd cancel instead."

"I would never have done that to you, well not unless there was a good enough reason."

"Okay then, let's go."

"Don't wait up for me," I said to Trisa, "and don't do anything crazy, okay?"

"Will you stop worrying Linda, and just go out on your date?" she replied.

Tony escorted me at to his car. It was beautiful, a Commodore club sport, it looked really good with all the spoiler kit and boot wing. It was a lovely shade of blue, this was all like a dream. Tony was being a real gentleman and it was a real pleasure to sit in his great car.

He drove us downtown. I was wondering where he might be taking us. Then all of a sudden we came to a halt. He got out, opened the door for me and told me to close my eyes. I wasn't too sure about it but I did it anyway. Tony walked me around the car then up the footpath. I was scared of tripping on something but he was very careful so that I didn't hear a door open and close, then he told me to open my eyes. It took a few seconds for me to adjust, then I realised we were in a theatre. Tony showed me to our seats than the show started. It was a dancing concert. The dancers were really great and then the next one came on and Tony pointed her out to me.

"Linda, see that girl with the brown hair on the left of the stage?"

"Yes," I said.

"Well that's my sister, Elizabeth."

"I never knew you had a sister."

"You never asked."

"How old is Elizabeth? Is she younger or older than you?"

"Elizabeth is younger, she's 18."

"I just realised I never asked you how old you are," I said.

"I'm 24. And you?"

"I am 17, going 18 this summer."

"Well then, there is six years between us. Does that bother you, Linda?"

"No, it shook me at first but not now. How about you?"

"Not at all, it's not your age I am worried about."

"What do you mean by that?"

"Well as long as you're not married, I am not. I like you and your age doesn't concern me."

The dancing finished, then he said, "Come on, it's time we got going."

"Where are we going now?"

"It's another surprise," he said.

This time, Tony pulled up outside a fancy looking restaurant.

"Shall we go in?" he said.

"Yes, of course."

He walked me through the restaurant and out onto the balcony and held the chair for me to be seated.

"Why thank you!" I said.

"Any time," he replied.

When the waitress came I looked at the menu and ordered the veal. Tony ordered chicken. When the food came it was wonderful. Afterwards we walked down to the beach behind the restaurant and we walked along with the moonlight reflecting off the water making it a perfect finish to the day and very romantic as well.

Tony took my hand in his as we walked along the sandy shore and all of a sudden he stopped and spun around in front of me he took me on his arms and bent down to kiss me. It took me by surprise but I kissed him back and it was a magical kiss. It lasted for a couple of minutes. Then Tony looked into my eyes.

"Linda, I know we've just met but it feels like I've known you for years. I'm sorry if I came on too strong but I really like you and would like to keep on seeing you. Would you like that, or would you need some time to think things through? It's all right with me, either way."

"Tony, you're so wonderful, you've given me the perfect evening. I do really like you. Yes, I would love to keep on seeing you. I'm so glad now that I agreed to come on this date with you and yes, I also think I need some time to think things through."

"That's fine Linda, we'll just take things slowly until you're ready," he said.

We walked further along the beach then we sat down on the sand. Tony sat behind me with his legs either side of me. I leaned back against his chest and he wrapped his arms around me. It was a lovely embrace, I could feel his chest moving in and out with every breath he took. I could smell his aftershave. I thought to myself that I'd remember that night for ever. Then Tony said it was getting late and that he'd better get me home.

On the way home I never wanted this night to end but I knew all good things had to come to an end sometime. When we got home Tony kissed me good night and said he would call me soon.

I walked in the door only to have Trisa pounce on me.

"So tell me, how did it all go?" she demanded.

"It was lovely," I replied. "The perfect evening, nothing went wrong. I really enjoyed it, to tell you the truth."

"Come on, come on," she squeaked. "Details! Don't leave me hanging. So what's he like? What did you to get up to?"

I must have been blushing as Trisa picked up on it right away.

"By that look, it was good," she said. "Tell me all about it."

"Well, Tony took me to the theatre where his sister Elisabeth was dancing. Then we went to dinner by the river and after we walked along the beach holding hands and then he kissed me."

"Wow! He kissed you! It does sound great. I'm jealous, I miss Lea already and he only left this morning."

"I'm sorry Trisa, I should have asked you to come instead of leaving you all alone."

"No, I would have been alone even if I did go. By the sounds of your night, I might have spoiled it all for you."

"Don't be silly, Trisa. You're my sister, I like being with you."

I was getting tired so I said good night and went to bed.

The next day I woke up and decided I would have to choose between Dave and Tony but which one, I didn't know. Dave was good-looking and I did meet him first. But then Tony was also good-looking and thinks about me a lot. And then again, I'd only just met both of them and didn't really know what to do. I had no idea.

Later on that day, both Tony and Dave came over to see me at the same time. It was so confusing and frustrating. I didn't know which one to talk to, what to say to either of them. In the end I said that I needed to make a decision and asked them what we should do.

Tony said, "Why don't you spend a couple of hours with one of us then a couple of hours with the other in the same day. That way you could compare your feelings and make a decision and in that way you will have had time to get to know us both. Hopefully it'll help you."

"Well I want first bid," Dave said.

It made me feel like a piece of meat hanging on the butcher's window like a prize waiting to be won.

"Okay then," said Tony. "I'll wait. Linda is worth waiting for."

*How sweet*, I thought.

Dave took me out in his car and we went to the beach. It was a nice day.

"Did you bring your bathers, Linda?" he asked.

"No, I didn't know I'd need them."

"Well, we'll have to find something else to do then."

We just walked along the beach, not really saying much at all and I was starting to get a bit bored.

"So what do you see in the guy, anyway?" asked Dave.

"He's very sweet, gentle, romantic and just a really nice guy."

"Still, I can't see why you even think that," replied Dave.

We walked along a little more then I decided to head back to the car. I told Dave I'd better be getting home now.

"Why, so you can spend time with that guy?"

"Yes I suppose so. Well, you made the deal."

"Yeah, I know. Well, come on then and I'll take you home."

When he dropped me off at home there was no sign of Tony yet, so I just said goodbye to Dave and went inside. I decided to change and shower before I went with Tony. Besides, I had sand all over me.

Tony arrived just as I was ready so we said goodbye to Trisa and left. I liked being with Tony and he did own a really nice car. He drove into town and I was wondering where he might be taking me this time. Just as I was thinking that, Tony pulled up again. He got out, walked around and opened my door for me. He led me into a Chinese restaurant where we had dinner, it really was lovely. Tony never let me pay for anything. Afterwards he took me on a ferry ride, it was beautiful. The moon lit up the water and you could see all the buildings reflected on the sea surface.

"Linda, look down there," he said.

"Oh Tony, it's beautiful!" I said. There were dolphins swimming alongside the boat. Things always seemed magical whenever Tony was around, I thought. But finally we went back to the car.

"Are you ready to go home yet, Linda, or would you like to stay with me for a little while longer?" he asked.

"I'd love to stay awhile longer, if it's okay with you," I replied

**48**

"It's fine with me," he said. "In fact, I was hoping that you'd like to stay."

So we stopped by the beach then we had an ice cream and walked all along the sand. Why did it feel so different walking on the beach with Tony as against Dave? Tony held my hand again, it made me feel like there were butterflies dancing all over my body. I felt so safe and warm whenever I was with them. I never wanted to go home again, but I knew eventually I'd have to.

"Linda, would you like to come back to my place for a while? But I don't want to push you, and if you don't, that's fine with me."

"Tony, I think that I'd better go home. Trisa would worry not only that, I'd need to sort out what I'm going to do. I'm sorry if I've offended you."

"Not at all," he said. "I understand completely. After all, it is your choice and I accept that."

He took me home and we kissed again before I got out. When I went inside, I didn't see Trisa so I went upstairs and she wasn't anywhere to be found. I assumed she'd gone out to one of her parties. I knew it couldn't last long.

When I woke up in the morning, I heard some noise coming from downstairs, so I went to see what was happening and saw it was Mum.

"Hi darling," Mum said. "How was your weekend?"

"It was great," I said. "I met two guys."

"Yes, and what happened? Who are these two guys?"

"Their names are Tony and Dave," I replied. "I went on dates with both of them. they both like me and I like them both, now they want me to choose between them."

"And which one would you choose?"

"Neither of them. I haven't decided how I am supposed to choose between them. What if I choose the wrong one?"

"Well Linda, I know it's very hard but you will still need to make a choice. After all, they won't wait around for you forever. But all I can tell you is to make sure you choose carefully. Because if you make the wrong choice, then they may not want you back. The thing you need to do is to sit down and make a list of all the good and bad things about each one of, how each one makes you feel when you are with them and apart from and whose company you enjoy the most and above all, how they treat you. Just go with your head and you'll make the right choice."

"Thank you, Mum," I said

"I just hope I've helped you and not confused you," she said. "Then again, you should never rush anything that means so much to you. After all, I'd hate for you to make the wrong choice, for all for my input to destroy your true feelings. I think you already really know will you've chosen, you just need time to think it through."

"You know Mum, you always seem so wise. How do you do it?"

"With a lot of practice and heartbreaks," Mum said. "Just remember, I was once young and single just like you."

"I know. Thanks again, Mum."

"Any time Linda, just remember I'm always here if you need to talk."

"I'm glad you are," I said.

A couple of days passed and I hadn't heard or seen Tony or Dave. I gathered that they were waiting on my decision. Finally, I decided who it would be. All I had to do now was to tell them who I had chosen. The only thing was that I didn't want to offend or upset anyone but I knew it was now time to let them know, so I went to see Dave first.

"Hi Dave," I said as he opened his door to me. "How have things been going?"

"Okay Linda," he replied. "I thought I'd give you some space. I knew you'd come and see me sooner or later, so tell me, what did you decide?"

"Now Dave, no matter what I decide, I would like it if we could all still be friends."

"Of course Linda, you're too nice a person to lose."

"Well, my decision was very hard and I'm still a little uncertain but I'm going to stay with Tony. I'm so sorry Dave, I really do like you a lot and it's a shame that things worked out the way they did."

"It's fine, I kind of knew it anyway. After all we've had fun together, maybe next time."

"Maybe," I said. "Now I'd like it if we could just stay friends. How do you feel about that? I'd understand."

"Of course I want to stay friends," he said.

I was so relieved that Dave had taken it so well, then again I wondered if it was a front. Well, there wasn't really anything between us to start with, it wasn't as if we'd kissed or anything. Actually I didn't even feel that bad about it anymore. All I had to do now was to let Tony know, I just hoped that he hadn't changed his mind. After all, I hadn't heard from him for a while.

I pulled up at Tony's house and just as I was about to get out of my car, I saw him walk out of the house with another woman. They kissed and embraced. I got so mad that I started my car and drove off but just as I was leaving, Tony looked up and waved me back but instead, I just kept on driving.

A couple of weeks passed and I hadn't seen Tony. I felt so stupid, thinking that he had really like me and that I had fallen for him. In the meantime, Trisa and Lea were always together. Mum approved of them dating and Mum thought Lea was a decent guy.

Our party was coming up. Mum had been organising it all. She said that she wanted to do it because now we were growing up and soon we could even end up moving out and having our own life. Mum always said that she wouldn't know what to do with herself when we had gone. I could never picture us not living with Mum, she was the best.

As it was getting closer to the party, Trisa started feeling a bit sick. Mum thought she'd just caught a bug or fatigue from all the late nights Trisa was having. We hardly saw much of her anymore, she and Lea were inseparable.

One night I walked into the bathroom and it sounded like Trisa was crying. When I opened the door she was vomiting and weeping.

"Trisa, I you okay?" I cried.

"No Linda I'll never be okay ever again."

"Why, what do you mean, you'll never be okay again?"

"Oh Linda, promise me you won't tell, please promise me."

"Okay. But first, what am I promising for? What's happened?"

"You remember Lea's party we went to?"

"You, what about it?"

"Well, he was such a gentleman, so romantic, the evening was going so well. Anyway, remember I was late getting home that night?"

"You, I remember."

"Well Linda, I slept with Dave."

"I thought you might have fallen asleep with him, after all you were inseparable that night."

"What I mean Linda, is that Lea and I made love."

"Oh Trisa, you didn't!"

"I did and there's more."

"What more could there be?" I asked.

"Lots more! Linda, I'm pregnant."

"Oh Trisa, are you sure?"

"Yes I am sure, I saw the doctor today, it's for real all right."

I was lost for words for a minute then I gathered myself together again.

"Congratulations!" I hugged her and she had a little smile. "What are you going to do?" I continued. "Are you going to keep it?"

"I don't know what I'll do. I thought about keeping it, I couldn't get rid of it, after all, it is part of me now."

"Does Lea know? Are you going to tell him?"

"No, I haven't told him yet, you're the only one who knows, but I'll have to tell him. I'm scared Linda, what will I do?"

"I think that you should tell Lea, after all, he's the father."

"But what if he leaves me and never wants to see me or the baby again?"

"If he's any sort of decent bloke, he'll stay with you. He should love you even more because now you'll have two people to love."

"You think so?"

"I do," I said. "When are you going to tell Mum?"

"I don't know, probably after the party."

She shook herself and turned to me. "So Linda, who did you end up choosing out of Tony and Dave anyway? I'd been meaning to ask you but never seemed to have the time."

"Actually, I chose Tony."

"So will he be coming to the party?"

"No, I don't think so." I began to feel angry again.

"Why not?" asked Trisa curiously.

"Because I never had the chance to tell him."

"How come?"

"Well, I went to his place and just as I was going to get out of my car, he walked out and kissed and hugged a woman."

"So didn't you want to see she was?"

"No, I just left. Tony tried to call me back but I just kept on going."

"So what sort of kiss was it?" Trisa asked.

"Just a quick peck on the cheek."

"Maybe it was just a friend," said Trisa

"I don't know, at the time I was too cranky to find out."

"Oh Linda, you poor thing. I'm sorry, I never realised."

"No, it's okay Trisa, after all, you've had your own problems."

"Still, I should have noticed."

"It's fine," I said.

The day of our party arrived. We were both very excited. We both loved the parties Mum threw for us. Everyone had arrived and the affair started. It was such a cool party. Mum gave Trisa and me a glass of wine each and we toasted each other's coming-of-age. Trisa hadn't told Mum about Lea yet, otherwise she'd never let her drink. Trisa was good however, she only had the one glass of wine all night.

It was getting late and people were leaving. Mum made sure nobody who had been drinking would be driving.

Somebody tapped me on the shoulder and when I turned around I saw it was Tony and he was holding a present.

"This is for you Linda," he said. "Happy birthday. I've missed you."

"Thank you, Tony," I said. "How did you know it was my birthday?"

"Trisa told me," he said.

"When did you see Trisa?"

"She came over last night and told me what had happened. I'm so sorry I didn't come ask you the other day. I thought that you might not have wanted to see me anymore, that you'd changed your mind, so I decided to give you your space."

"Tony, I came to see you to let you know that I'd chosen to stay with you, but when I got there, I saw you kiss and cuddle a girl, so I thought you didn't want to wait around for me anymore that you'd already moved on with your life."

"Linda, if you would have wanted, you would have noticed it was Elizabeth and me saying goodbye to each other."

I felt a mixture of shock and pleasure.

"Oh how stupid of me, I'm so sorry, I should have thought."

"Never mind, it's all in the past, I've come to ask you if you'd like to start being my girlfriend and make it official?"

"Oh yes, Tony I'd love that!"

Tony and I kissed and embraced each other. It seemed as though we been standing there forever, when suddenly I heard somebody clearing their throat behind me so I turned to see who it was and found it was Mum. So I introduced her to Tony. They got on really well, she approved of Tony and said she thought I'd made the right choice.

Dad rang up that evening and wished us a happy birthday. We didn't hear from Dad very much, but it was nice to get this call from him.

Later that night, Trisa told Mum she was pregnant. Mum asked her if Lea knew yet. Trisa said she'd told him that night and he said he had to go home and have some time to himself to think about it. Mum wasn't too pleased but she congratulated Trisa and told her she would always be there for her and the baby.

The next day Trisa had a doctor's appointment. When she came back she was glowing. Mum asked Trisa how it had gone and was everything all right.

"Yes Mum, even better," said Trisa. "I'm pregnant with twins!"

Mum just smiled and gave her a big hug and said, "All the more to love."

I congratulated Trisa and we talked about the baby for hours, what sort of things to buy, what names she'd pick, and about going looking for baby things together. The only thing that was really bugging Trisa was whether or not Lea would still love her.

Lea turned up later that day and Trisa told him that there were going to have twins and Lea was over the moon. He was so happy that they were having twins, he said it would take some time to adjust, but that they'd manage somehow. It was good to see that he loved Trisa so much and didn't just run and hide from his responsibilities.

Tony and I got on so well, we were thinking about moving in together. Trisa and Lea said that they wanted to wait until the babies were born before they decided whether or not to move in together. They was such a lovely couple.

www.ingramcontent.com/pod-product-compliance
Lightning Source LLC
Chambersburg PA
CBHW061457170626
46811CB00004B/1553